Granny lives about a million miles away, in a place called Koala Lumpur. It's too far to walk, so they're all going to fly there in an aeroplane.

Kai sings lots of nice, loud songs, so that
       Daddy doesn't fall asleep while he's driving.

At long last, they arrive at . . .

. . . the Airport!
There are planes everywhere.

Most planes
don't have teeth.

This plane's called a Jumbo Jet,
because it's as big as an elephant.

The first thing the Koalas have to do is Check In.
That means showing your tickets and passports
to the person at the check-in desk. Everyone's
in a rush and there's a long queue.

CLAW JET
TO
CATMANDU

This is Kai's passport.
He's had it since he was a baby.

KAI
KOALA

PASSPORT

This ostrich has
lost her ticket.

This porcupine's
getting a bit prickly.

And this turkey's
flight is delayed
until Christmas.

2 FLEASY JET TO NEAR PAWTUGAL

3 BEARAIR TO KOALA LUMPUR

Kai is brilliant at pushing the trolley.
He's less good at making it stop.

Finally, the Koalas reach the top of the queue.
Their suitcases bump along the conveyor belt,
through the hatch and into the Bag Room.

You're not allowed to go with them,
even though it looks really fun.

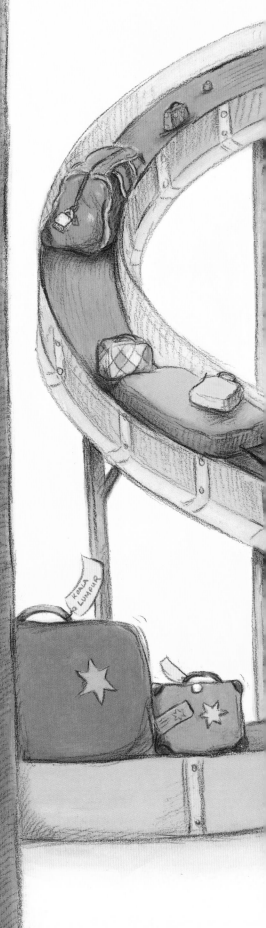

LUGGAGE
SCANNER

Bob works in the Bag Room
making sure the right suitcases
end up on the right planes.

His back's killing him today,
and he could do with a
cup of tea.

Next, everyone has to go through Security.

All the bags are x-rayed to see what's inside them, because there are some things you're not allowed to take on a plane.

These are some of the things you can't take with you:

Water pistols

Fireworks

Sharp objects

Some passengers have their pockets searched.

Others have to take off their belts and shoes. Then everyone queues up to walk through the metal detector.

It's a bit of a squeeze for a hippo.

Oops!

It's important to put your belt on again afterwards, or your trousers can fall down.

At long last, the Koalas arrive in the Departure Lounge.
That's where you wait while your plane is getting ready.
Mummy wants to go shopping and Daddy wants a
snack, but first Kai needs to leapfrog a rabbit.

Mummy tries on a bikini.

Daddy buys
Granny some perfume.

Next it's time for lunch. Sharon makes herself a spaghetti hat.
Kai's sandwich can fly like an aeroplane.

There's a good view of the runway
from the café window.

Kai counts the planes.
He can see nine planes,
one helicopter and a space rocket.

CARROT AIR

Angela is the Air Traffic Controller. It's her job to make sure the planes don't bump into each other.

A space rocket is looping-the-loop in the middle of the runway. Angela tells the pilot that he's just showing off and to stop it immediately.

There's just time for a nap after lunch.
Daddy definitely snores the loudest.

All of a sudden, they're
woken up by a very noisy
announcement:

"This is the FINAL CALL for
the Koala Family flying to Koala Lumpur!
Make your way IMMEDIATELY to Gate Two!"

Oh no! They're going to miss their flight!

Kai and Sharon shout, "Wheeee!" to make Mummy and Daddy run faster.

It's a long way to the plane.
Daddy runs his fastest, but
Mummy's still in the lead.

Groundhog the Ground Marshall is waiting
to guide the aeroplane on to the runway.

He signals to Mummy that she's dropped her new bikini!

Groundhog waves two paddles to send signals to the pilot.
This is what his signals mean:

Turn Right   Proceed   Stop!!!   Do a Dance

They board the plane just in time – phew!
They've only just got their seatbelts fastened,
when the plane's engines start up with a ROAR!

They're about to take off!

The plane hurtles along the runway, then . . .

. . . lift off!

They're soaring above the clouds.

This is the Cockpit, where Captain Scottie
and Co-Pilot Pink fly the plane. It takes ages
to learn how to use all those knobs and dials.

Once they're up in the air, the Cabin Crew can start serving dinner.
Some passengers have Special Dietary Requirements,
which means they eat something different.

This skunk has ordered
a smelly meal,

and the rabbits have gone
for the vegetarian option.

Aeroplane meals come in lots of little pots on a tray.

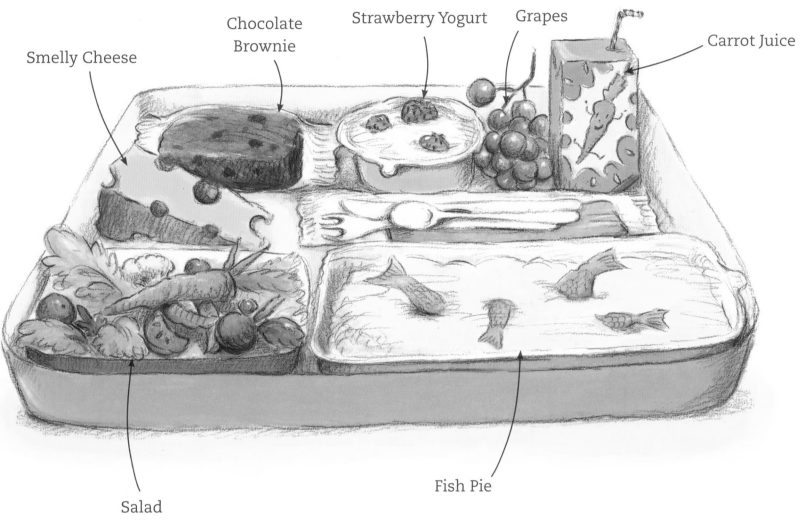

Smelly Cheese

Chocolate Brownie

Strawberry Yogurt

Grapes

Carrot Juice

Salad

Fish Pie

It can be tricky opening all those pots.
Juice cartons are especially squirty.

Squirt!

After dinner, Kai and Sharon keep themselves busy
while Mummy and Daddy have a nap.

First they try out their new felt-tip pens.

Then they sing all their favourite songs.

They're just in the middle of
a new dance routine, when . . .

. . . Captain Scottie makes an announcement.

"Please take your seats for landing!"

It's exciting looking out of
the window as the plane
comes in to land.

It's less exciting cleaning
felt pen off your face.

At last they've arrived!
It's very hot in Koala Lumpur –

especially for penguins.

Inside the Arrivals Hall, the Koalas
spot Granny waving at them.

But first they have to pick up their suitcases.

Koala Family!

FLIGHT 1
BEAR AIR

Those baggage carousels
go faster than you'd think.

Finally, it's time to head off to . . .

. . . Granny's party!

And what an amazing party it is.

Great dancing, Daddy Koala!

For Hannah Rentta, who lives about
a million miles away, and for Pilot John.

First published in 2015 by Alison Green Books
An imprint of Scholastic Children's Books
Euston House, 24 Eversholt Street, London NW1 1DB
A division of Scholastic Ltd
www.scholastic.co.uk
London – New York – Toronto – Sydney – Auckland
Mexico City – New Delhi – Hong Kong

HB ISBN: 978 1407 14732 1
PB ISBN: 978 1407 14733 8

1 3 5 7 9 8 6 4 2

The moral rights of Sharon Rentta have been asserted.

Papers used by Scholastic Children's Books
are made from wood grown in sustainable forests.